Nameless

Illustrated Short Story

Riza Lubasheva

Published by

RCreator Press

Cover design by Kayl Studio.

ISBN 978-0-6458332-5-6

Published by RCreator Press

*Dedicated to
My Writing Center Colleagues*

Thank you for encouraging me to write more often and better than before.

Table of Contents

ALAX

Prologue

Aigaion changed. The townspeople made a statement when they elected Ajax as our new leader, "We accept anyone." Despite being born here, I had no say in the matter because I was still learning to speak at the time. However, soon I would be raised in that sentiment and cheerfully accept it. Legend says that Ajax's birthplace tore from war. His mother sought asylum here until she could get back on her feet, but they never left. This tale spread by the people cemented the success of his inspirational campaign, but he never spoke a word of his past only of Aigaion's future in continued prosperity.

Some townsfolk considered his methods paradoxical. Ajax proudly proclaimed his anti-war sentiments, yet he built Aigaion's military from nothing. He also decreed construction of large stone walls with one entrance into the city. When I turned sixteen, I started training with all the other young boys under Ajax himself. I remember Ajax's first words he spoke directly to me, "I trust you." He started with those words to gain my full attention. "That's why I am giving you the most important task. Guard the gate," He ordered.

Dimitris and I watched the progressive construction of Aigaion's walls, never predicting they'd one day be ours to defend. On my first day, I smiled at him, "Still following in your footsteps." He smiled back, but it faded away void of his previous childlike laughter. He took Ajax's words closer to heart than I did. Often, we'd argue at the gate about the significance of our position. Dimitris adamantly defended Ajax's opinion, while I reminded Dimitris that we never needed a military before.

I believed the walls were a big enough expression of Ajax's intention of never expanding our borders. The big, hefty stone imprinted the land Aigaion owned. We had great relations with our neighbors. Our agricultural output let us trade our abundance of food for anything neighboring villages had to offer. During famine, we fed thousands of our neighbors in need. I did not understand why our small farming village needed a military, let alone thick stone walls. I held too much trust in our safety, while I thought Dimitrius held too little.

Dimitrius heavily respected the leaders of our village. He often stayed chatting with the blacksmith, who knew Ajax more personally, to get inspired from more stories about Ajax's past. He held so much loyalty to Ajax. Dimitrius agreed with me that we may never use our military or need our walls, but he adamantly believed they were a necessity. Despite our little arguments in ideals, he stayed like a big brother to me.

Ajax continued to put his trust in me, but I continued to distrust his plans, until the rumors started. At first, I couldn't believe Dodasa's actions. I naïvely updated Dimitris as if it was nothing, but simple gossip. We both continued to boast our brave faces to everyone, yet underneath we worried our time of military play would end. During this time, I started to understand the sentiment Ajax and Dimitris shared. The military and walls weren't built to send an intimidating message of toughness. Ajax created them so a history of war would not repeat itself or even start. His defensive actions bore a new leader in Aigaion.

During this new shift in our history, another child seeking refuge appeared. At first Dimitris and I were startled by her. She approached without a sound. Her footsteps were quieter than a ghost's touch. I recognized her only from my vision. She stood stiffly composed with both her palms resting on Aigaion's only sign. I approached first eager to aid a lost child, but she remained unresponsive. The most I knew of her was that she came from across the bridge. On the days she appeared, not a single sound exited her lips,

not even a

NAME

LESS

1

Chapter 1

"Come home!" the woman demanded as her hand gripped my wrist, attempting to pull me off the bridge. The place she ignorantly labeled as home restricted any sound produced from my lips. There, I slumbered in the closet to remain unseen from the public eye. A small, miscalculated movement garnered severe punishment. On every window and wall supporting that house, I often imagined steel bars, the only thing that the prison lacked.

"Hand over our daughter!" the woman's husband screamed in Ajax' face. As he turned to me, I tugged my wrist out of the woman's claws and returned to the center of the bridge. I clutched my wrist as it throbbed. Ajax stood two heads taller than the couple and planted himself between us. "How dare you join a village in war! At home, you're safe away from all this conflict," they repeated. I remained silent, but they refused to stand by while the property stolen from them walked away. The couple dashed behind Ajax and reached out their hands to get any hold on me. However, Evander pulled my hood from the other end of the bridge. My body dropped into Eleni's arms, as Dimitris and Colin forcefully pushed the couple away.

Eleni propped me up and gently took my hand. We followed Evander away from the commotion at the bridge. When my head tugged back, I saw Ajax dragging the aggressors away from the bridge. "They are right, you know. If you go with them, you won't get slaughtered with us." I kept silent as I responded with a simple nod. My prison escape succeeded, and the three of us peacefully returned to my true home.

The first time I escaped from my birthplace, I ran until I hit a sign on a stone wall that bordered a beautiful pasture. "Welcome to Aigaion!" the sign celebrated. Outside stood two guards laughing with each other until they spotted my stunted frame shivering. Before I fled, they approached me with concern written on their faces. "Where are your parents?" they interrogated. A word never left my lips, yet the taller one, Dimitris, hauled a stool over and propped it up in front of their station.

"You can sit here if you like," the other guard, Colin, added. Eventually, I accepted after standing at a distance for a while. They tried to involve me in their conversation, but I stayed silent. When the sun dimmed orange, Colin brought food for the three of us. They placed a soft round loaf in my hands. I sunk my teeth into the freshest bread I had ever eaten as they continued to discuss the matters of Aigaion.

"Rumor is negotiations aren't going so well," Colin stated.

"There are no negotiations to be made," Dimitris replied sternly. "Dodasa's insane if they think heavily overstepping like this is acceptable."

The two of them briefly glanced at me as I scarfed down their gift.

"Time for you to go home, little one. Our shift's over now." Dimitris informed as he gestured for me to get up. Colin grabbed the stool and the two of them disappeared inside the walls. I dared not follow them then, but the next time I tumbled into those pristine cream-colored stones, they invited me inside. Each building faced inward and welcomed passersby through their doors. Dimitris and Colin continued their conversations as I followed behind them.

"War? Where are you hearing these ridiculous rumors? I refuse to believe Ajax suggested that" Dimitris scoffed.

"He did not suggest it. Dodasa declared war on us! It's official news," Colin clarified.

Their words reached my ears, but the lush beauty of the meadow which Aigaion sat on stole my focus. The buildings never intruded on the rich nature that the villagers cultivated inside their walls. Still, time barely passed before I met Ajax. An intimidating man with a foreboding presence interrupted the guard's conversation. "Who's this girl with you?" he inquired, pointing to me.

"No clue, sir." Colin answered.

"She may be mute," Dimitris jested.

Ajax kneeled next to me and asked, "What's your name, child?"

I just shook my head in response.

Ajax chuckled. Then, he extended his hand and properly introduced himself, "Welcome to my Aigaion! Enjoy your stay; just don't make trouble, you hear?" I shook his hand and enthusiastically nodded. Soon everyone knew of me. The time between my visits grew shorter and shorter. No one in the village yelled at me to go away, and some even gave me spare items to make toys out of. They fed me, sometimes clothed me. Best of all they gave me a name.

"Hera!" Evander proudly announced, while sharpening a sword.

"Hera?" I questioned.

Evander, the blacksmith, shocked, replied to my first words, "Do you like it? It kills me that no one refers to you by name. Even if it's not your real name, can I call you Hera?"

"Mhmm." I nodded as I tried to forge a sword like him.

On the days I sneaked off to that beautiful pasture, I tinkered with my stash of objects at Evander's establishment, then watched over Dimitris and Colin as they joined the rest of the warriors to train with Ajax. Occasionally, I ran down to them with the sword I made and insisted on inclusion. "I can do that too!" I shouted.

"Hera, this is very important. We need to prepare and not be distracted. Please go back to Evander for the day," Ajax pleaded.

The last time I appeared at Aigaion's gate, the skin around my eye turned black and swollen. Dried blood stained my shirt. I shivered again. Before I entered, I composed myself and made sure no trace of tears imprinted my face. I never knew when returning to the village would end, so I made the most of every day. I walked up to the gate and smiled. "Hi Colin! Where's Dimitris?"

"Woah! Are you okay?" Colin reacted.

"I'm fine, as always," I replied.

He knelt in front of me and asked, "Did a bully get you again?"

I nodded yes.

"Do you want to talk about it?"

I shook my head no.

Eventually, Colin could not ignore it. Again, I cleaned up as best I could, but the confrontation from the night prior violently painted itself on my canvas. That day progressed with a greater amount of interrogation, "What happened? Who did this to you? Why won't you say anything?" I grew quiet like before. Colin asked Dimitris to escort me home safely. Dimitris accompanied me home despite my insistence that he return. When we arrived, I asked him to stand a decent distance away from the house. He watched as I crawled into the back window and remained silent. The next time I approached them Colin exclaimed, "Stay with us!"

Dimitris interjected, "Idiot, she's better off not involved with our conflict."

"I'd like to," I replied with my eyes shining at them.

"No, you don't understand," Dimitris continued. "All of us could be gone tomorrow."

"She's just a child!" Colin expressed.

"She's old enough to make an informed decision!" Dimitris shouted.

He knelt next to me, put his hand on my shoulder, and looked me in the eye. "Dodasa's coming any day now to take our land. You should not get involved in that stupid mess, but..." He resumed. "But it's your choice, kid. We'll stand by whatever you decide. However, know that Aigaion could be gone the next time you visit, and you'd be safe."

"I understand," I affirmed.

The day I joined Aigaion could never be described as pretty. The homeowner of my previous residence bent my nose in as I tried to leave. Both the adults ran after me as I crossed the river to Aigaion. After the altercation, Evander's wife, Eleni, attended to my wounds as usual, except this was the last time she would treat me for insignificant black eyes. After she finished, I went and played with Helios, Evander's new son. We shared a room, and I assisted in any way I could, to show my gratefulness to Evander and Eleni.

In my new home, I beamed. I brought Helios with me everywhere. I made toys for him out of my tinker box. Together, the four of us, Evander, Eleni, Helios, and I, ate dinner every night, where I got time to show Evander everything I made that day. Since living in the village, I did everything I could to help. I repaired flower beds, installed new door hinges, entertained the little ones, and tried to give advice to Colin and Dimitris's training. However, Ajax often had to pull me away for being "distracting." I wanted my home to stand strong.

As I observed it every day, it surprised me how tight-knit and friendly Aigaion seemed, since two thirds of the population formed the militia. My life completely flipped after finding my home. They gave me a name. They welcomed me. They allowed me to lay peacefully in the flower fields without worry of being yelled at. They provided me freedom to pursue inventing and improve the village with my ideas. Colin and Dimitris often helped find places for my inventions to shine throughout the village. Then, I would explain how they worked to Helios even though he could not form words. They valued me. A stupid war could not make me lose that.

Unfortunately, that day came. The modified horns I installed sounded louder than ever before, and all the women and children fled to the central hall, except for me. Despite Ajax screaming at me to go with them, I grabbed my sword and followed Colin to the gate. Dimitris waited for Colin there, and he prevented me from going further. I was no match for him, and Evander dragged me with them to safety. Eleni watched over me with hawk eyes and attempted to distract me by playing games with Helios. Evander periodically left the hall and returned with whispers he only gave to the elders.

The door opened again slowly, as Evander fell to the floor forming a puddle of tears. "We lost," he whispered. I charged for the gate. Eleni chased after me leaving Helios screaming in tears. She begged me to stay put. She could not stop me. Upon opening the gate, my eyes met the corpses of Colin, Dimitris, Ajax, and the rest of my friends.

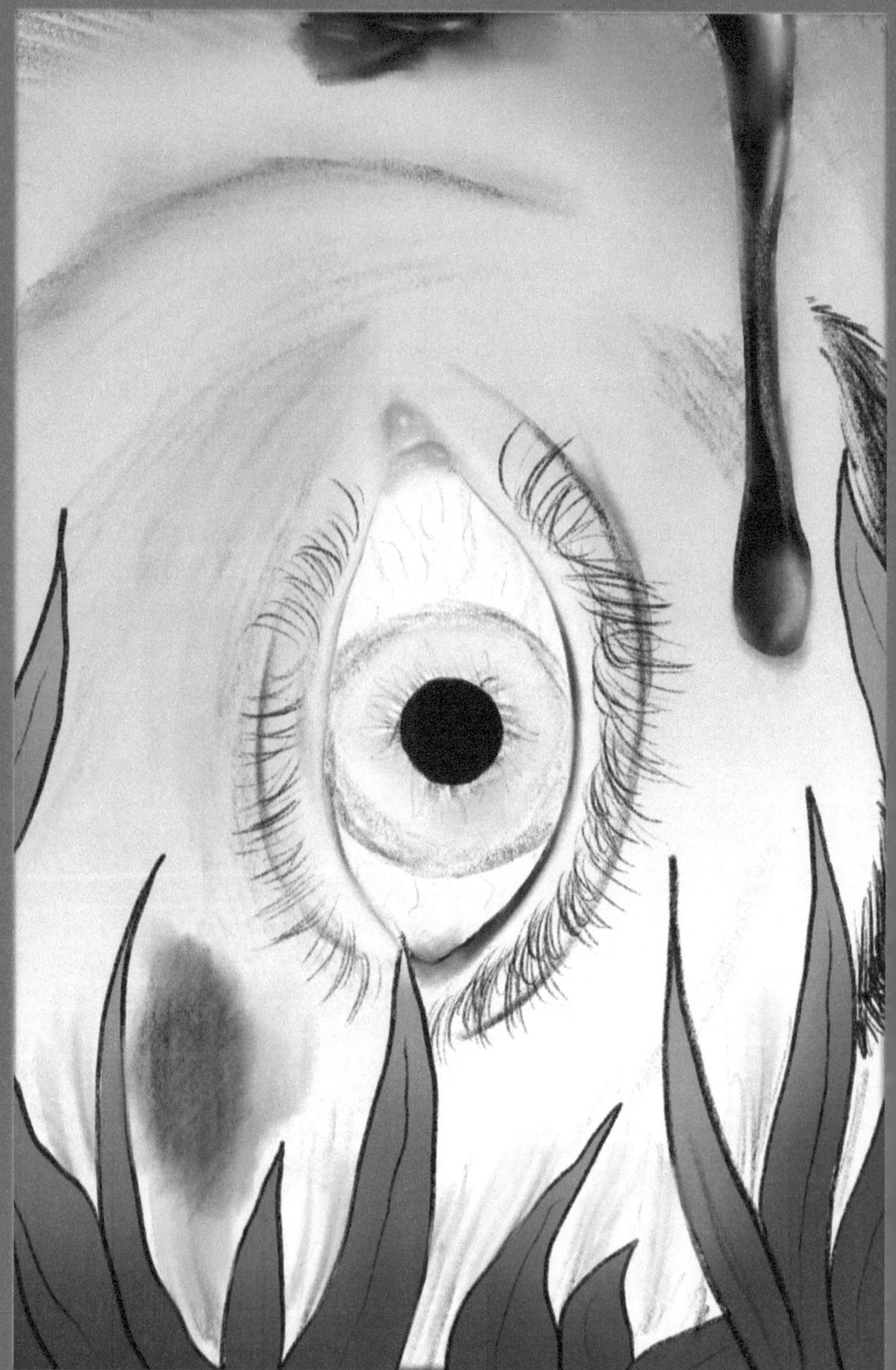

Chapter 2

"Leave!" the stranger uttered, "Since you have no ties to the village you can flee to safety." I scoffed at her and said, "This village is not just their home, its mine too; I will never leave my home." She smiled at me and said, "Then I will definitely need your help."

She appeared after the incident that dyed the outside stone walls red and covered my eyes. Her hands directed me back inside, where Eleni smothered me with a tearful hug. When I regained my composure, a tall woman wearing an ornate white cloak that shielded her eyes stood in front of me. She held a note that came from the other side of the gate, and her long black hair fell over it. "We have five days," she stated. Then, the stranger handed the note to Eleni as I remained in her arms. The note stated Dodasa would claim the land in 5 days and prepare it for their taking. Upon reading, I clenched my hands in rage.

"I can save you all!" The stranger promised. "But, not without Hera," she spoke while turning to me.

She referred to my inventions, the mechanisms I made for the village, the intricate toys I made for Helios, and the weapons Evander taught me how to forge. She called on me to create a defense for Aigaion. I smiled. That's all I ever wanted to do. The next few days, I poured myself into my mechanisms. I crafted a variety of weapons that were deadly, yet easy to use. Some I had heard of before, like catapults, and others I imbued with my creativity. The violent intent of the weapons I created did not cross my mind, as I saw them as nothing more than defense measures. The stranger gathered the remaining able-bodied adults and trained them on how to use my creations.

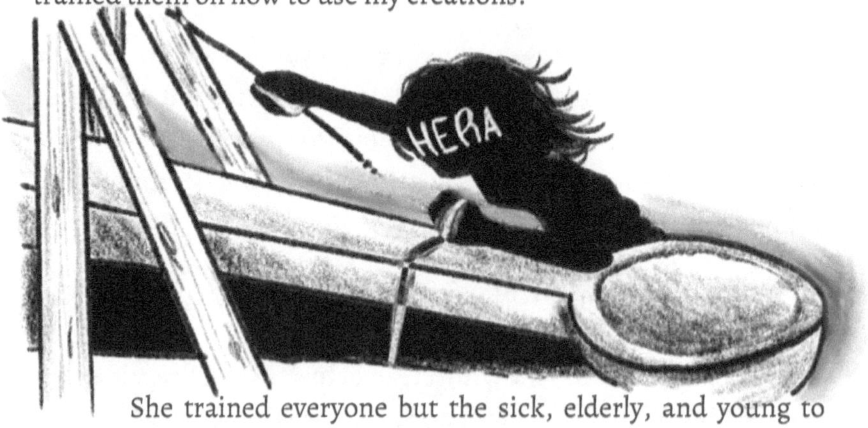

She trained everyone but the sick, elderly, and young to fight. She lumped me in with the young category, so I was useless to her. Because she viewed me as young and weak, I had to get on my knees and beg, "Let me fight with the others!" The outsider denied me, no matter how much I pleaded. Though, she allowed me to be there when training started to show them how everything worked. However, when she pushed me away from her lessons after, my face tightened up in frustration. The object of my desire stood as the only action the village forbade me from pursuing. I wanted to fight. I wanted to get stronger. I wanted to protect my home. That desire stayed unfulfilled because Evander, Eleni, and this new outsider denied it. Knowing my wish, they put me under watch to ensure that it would never come to pass.

They forgot about the years of masterful evasion that brought me to them. Despite their restrictions, I disobeyed their cruel orders. I would not let them stop me from fulfilling my purpose. I trained due to my many memories of grief for the corpses we buried. I fondly reminisced about Dimitris reprimanding Colin for not following Ajax's instructions closely and using me as an example for someone who earnestly listened to every lesson. Ajax used to praise my form and will to fight while forcefully pulling me back to Evander. They called my name and encouraged me, despite not wanting me to join their fight.

"Hera, you are the most determined citizen of Aigaion, but you are not a warrior," Ajax would repeat again and again.

"I can fight. I can become a warrior like them. I will prove them wrong," I whispered to myself. I continued to increase my strength whenever I could. I did not know if my tears came from reliving those memories or the searing pain from my fingers clutching the sword I swung for hours. Every day before the next calamity, I worked the best I could, no matter the toll. Despite my hand wanting to peel off, I continued with glee. I needed to get stronger. I needed to stop feeling defenseless. I needed to protect the family who named me.

Eventually, Evander allowed me to exit the gate again. I brought an old stool to prop up next to the gate and just reminisce for a little bit. I placed my hand on the red stone walls, questioning where those two last stood. We already buried all the corpses but had yet to hold a ceremony or decorate graves. I wondered what their final thoughts might have been. The sound of Evander hauling over a couple of my heavier defense mechanisms ended my short break. In preparation for the Day of Calamity, the people of Aigaion equipped the walls with my weapons.

Finally, the Day of Calamity arrived. Everyone stood ready to defend our home, even though death knocked at the door. Dodasa crossed the bridge, expecting us to sit defenseless while they carved their name into our land. The horns screamed the same as before. Our guardian, the stranger, directed everyone to their positions. I took Helios from Eleni as she left to fight with Evander. Before she left, she kissed both our foreheads and whispered, "Hera, Helios, my children, I love you. Everything will be okay. We will protect you." I loved hearing my name. Of all the words she said, "Hera," made me smile the most. I ran with Helios in my arms and left him with the elders as I again pursued the gate. I laid down the infant I had cared for as a brother for the last time and left the safe zone to fight. I fulfilled my task of getting everyone not fighting to safety, except me.

No one stood in my way this time, as everyone who could fought outside the walls. I grabbed my sword and lunged to defend my home. I readied myself for this since the beginning of the conflict. I wished to stand with Colin and Dimitris at the gates of the village and guard it with them. That wish can never be granted now. Like Colin and Dimitris, I aimed to get stronger and

HERA
HELIOS

stronger to protect our most valuable home. I think I understand what they must have thought on the day I last saw them; "Even if I die here, all my efforts were worth protecting this place."

Outside the gates existed a river of bloodshed. The weapons I created hit many of Dodasa's men, and they contemplated retreat. I stood on the battlefield among our newly trained warriors. However, when Evander saw me, he attempted to bring me back to the gate once more, but I ran from him into the enemy. "Hera! Stay back!" he yelled. I smiled, "I will not!" as I finally got to protect Aigaion with my own hands.

Upon my entry, I disrupted everyone's rhythm with their shock of a child coming to the rescue. My eyes met those of our guardian. Her face showed a horrified expression, not the reaction I imagined. Evander and Eleni went hysterical. I continued to swing my blade at the enemies, forcing them away from the gate. Suddenly, a hand grabbed onto me and interrupted my movements. The hand belonged to Evander. He grabbed my shoulders and forced me to face him. He cried, "Hera! You don't understand! We are not fighting to protect Aigaion or our land. We are protecting you." The enemies surrounding us began to run away as the familiar sound of one of my projectiles played. I reacted. I pushed Evander as hard as I could and sent him flying a couple feet away from me. The last thing I heard was his scream, "Hera!"

HERA

ELENI

Battle's End

After Dodasa completely retreated, everyone regrouped and celebrated. I approached Evander and Eleni curled over the frame of Aigaion's savior. Unfortunately, I failed as their guardian. Her eyes remained shut, but her heart still sang. Evander carried the girl back inside the walls for Eleni to address her wounds. They laid her in her bed waiting for her to smile again. As I followed them, I apologized, "I'm sorry, I couldn't keep my promise." Aigaion won at a cost. Surprisingly that cost was not life. Not even a single causality could be reported, but Hera was gone.

Chapter 3

I awoke in a strange place. The first pain I felt continued as a searing headache. My body lay on a soft cushion, all my wounds covered. Then, I heard a cry. Across from me stood a toddler bouncing in his crib, pointing at me with tears in his eyes. Soon, a woman arrived. Upon seeing me, she yelled a name; "Evander!" The woman approached and hugged me before taking a seat by my side. "How are you feeling?" she asked. Talking to strangers scared me, so I remained silent, not wanting to provoke any anger. A tall, bearded man entered with the biggest smile. He proceeded to soothe the crying toddler in his arms and took a seat next to the woman who called him. She continued to interrogate me. For most of the questions, I did not know the answers.

"Do you know where you are?"

No idea.

"Do you know who you are?

That never mattered.

"Your name?"

I never had one.

"Me?" the stranger concluded.

I remained silent.

Six pairs of eyes pierced mine with a faint look of horror. All but the toddler seemed to be holding back tears. The child tearfully extended his arms toward me waiting for a response. I stayed still, not wanting to do anything disallowed. At first, my mind confusingly wondered where my parents were. It took me too long to realize that they finally disowned me.

"Maybe she just needs some time, Eleni?" the man questioned.

"Maybe," the lady whispered.

The man put his hand on my head and looked me in the eye. "You rest up well now, you hear?"

Then, the three of them left me alone in the house, so they could share some news with the rest of this unusual village. It puzzled me as to why these two would care for me in their own home and not introduce themselves. Did this place not have a hospital, orphanage, or somewhere else I could be left to be forgotten.

It took me some time to move normally again. Surprisingly, the adults I stayed with allowed me to venture outside. Everywhere I wobbled, someone was there to lend me a hand, despite my silent protest. The people of this place, Aigaion, truly acted very oddly towards me.

WHO?
WHO?
WHO?

No one introduced themselves to me. They just stood there smiling and saying things like, "I'm so overjoyed that you are alright!" A few reached their arms out to me, but hesitated once they realized my indifferent reaction. The pair whose house I intruded never mentioned moving me elsewhere. I kept waiting for their patience with me to end, especially once I fully recovered, but that time never came.

I did not mind sharing a room with their son. He seemed to like me, but I wondered why they trusted me so much with their child. He often ran up to me extending his arms forward with a little jump. The most I ever reacted toward him was to gently place my hand on his head. The child would not leave me alone most of the time. He often put his clearly custom-made toys in my lap and pointed. He started leaving them around the house in obvious spaces I would see, so I had to return them. He always gave me the biggest smile as I brought the toys back to his palms.

Eventually, my caregivers hauled me to an Aigaion meeting. When the four of us entered, the villagers cheered. I guess those two must be some big shots in the community. After everyone gathered, a short measure of silence fell before a clear outsider arrived. Her long black hair dangled over her peculiar clothing that included a hood over her eyes which contrasted with the rest of her clothes. The people of Aigaion hung on to every one of her words.

Soon she approached me and took me by the hand. The stranger asked me similar questions to the ones I heard when I awoke.

"Do you remember this village? Your home?" she probed.

Aigaion did seem familiar. Maybe I visited a few times as a child, but I could not recall much. As for my home, I had no desire to return there. However, my response to her remained the same as always, not a single word left my tongue. The measure of silence resumed as she waited for me to answer anything. Her face painted a strong look of frustration. The stranger clenched her palms and broke the silence in a defeated voice as she turned to face the crowed, "I'm sorry I failed you." Then she stormed out and never appeared again to them.

The man I walked in with approached me and said in a similar tone, "Do you remember me?"

What a weird *stranger*, I thought. I grew to know him better while staying at his house and looking after his child, but why would someone even ask that question of someone they recently met. Again, I had no intention of angering them, so I replied with silence. The people of Aigaion approached me afterward and reacted similarly. It made me uncomfortable how suddenly everyone around me wanted to help, listen, and spend time with me.

Eventually, I ended that uncomfortableness. When my wounds left no impression on my body, and I returned to a normal state, I prepared to leave Aigaion. A strong desire dominated my mind. That vital urge begged me to act. I gathered my few belongings from under the bed and began to exit the house without a word. Then, the man stopped me and called for his wife. The thought of them preventing me from leaving frightened me. I sat down with them at the dining table as we shared our last meal. The couple went back and forth discussing my desire to leave. They never even considered a day like this would pass. Eventually, without needing any protest from me, they looked into my eyes and the woman answered, "It is your choice to leave. We will not force you to stay here."

"But please do not leave us without saying goodbye!" the man pleaded.

For the first time since I woke up, I smiled at them. I had no idea such kind people existed. They treated strangers better than family. However, their reaction turned my face back to normal. Both of their facades finally broke, and they began crying the same as their son. They tearfully asked, "Are you leaving now?"

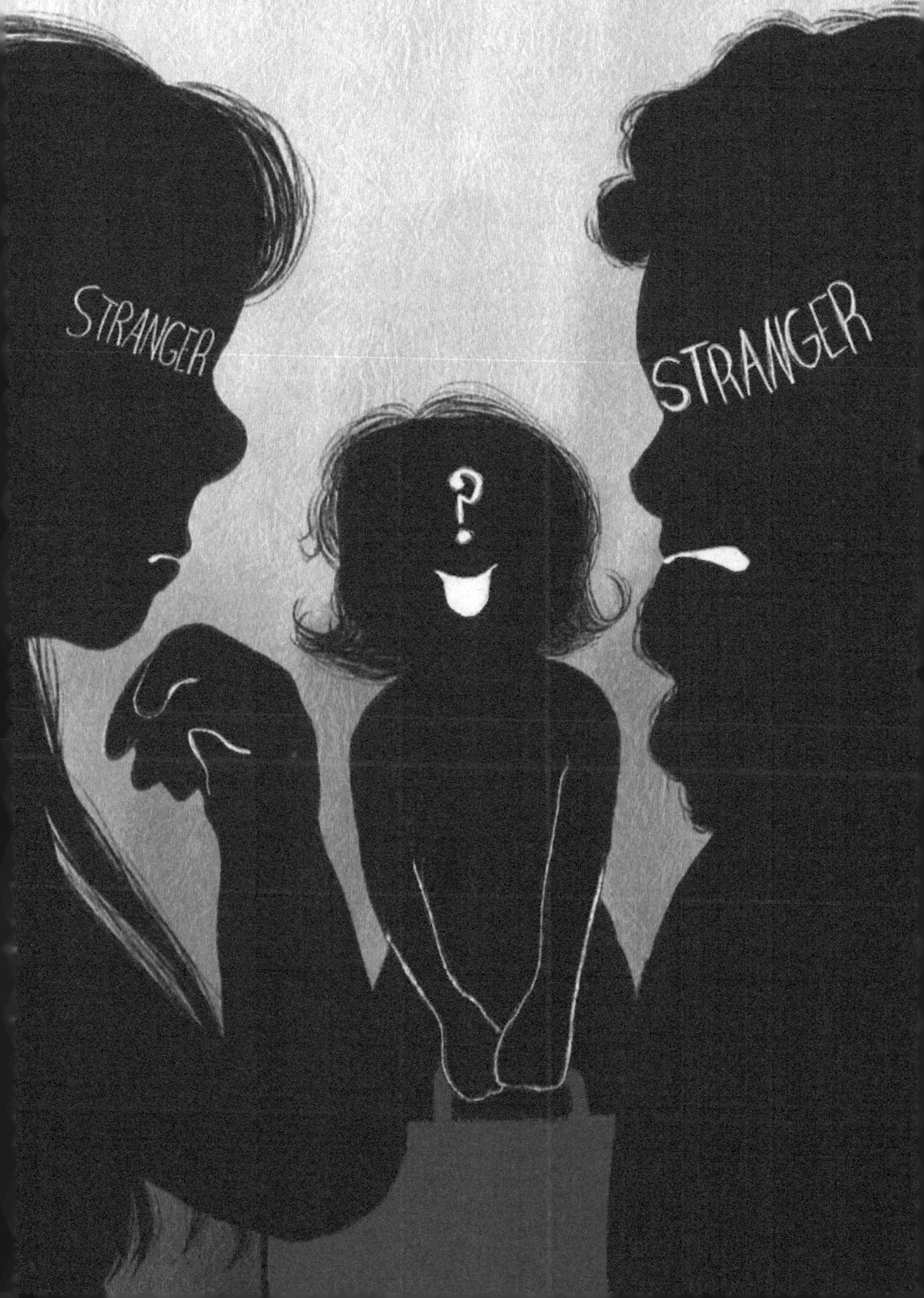

NAMELESS
STRANGER
STRANGER
?
NAMELESS

I nodded in return as I gathered my items. The lady left and returned with a bag of fresh loaves. Without asking, she placed them in my bag. Afterwards, her husband handed her their son, and picked up my bag. I gestured that I could take it just fine and that he did not need to help.

However, he responded, "It is the least I can do for you."

A few others followed the family and me to the gate. When we arrived, I took my bag from the weird stranger. I decided to say something to them, "Thank you." Then, I smiled out of a habit that escaped my memory and began to open the gate. He replied, "No, thank you for everything. Please come back soon." After I exited, I heard a thud as he fell to the ground sobbing more than I ever could. His wife ran out to me after I had already stepped a decent distance away. She turned her son toward me, and he waved goodbye, tears swelling in his eyes.

"Goodbye, Hera!" she screamed as I waved goodbye at a steady pace.

Outside, the wall displayed a completely different scene than the inside. Many large weapons positioned near the stone walls guarded Aigaion. Unlike the pristine inner walls, the stone that framed the gate presented many streaks of red. I considered it another odd trait of that location. The inside seemed like a peaceful environment, but beyond the walls illustrated something more that remained unknown to me.

I no longer had anywhere I could return to, but a mission captivated my motives. I needed to fight. I needed to get stronger, but I could not recollect why. That thought tainted my brain. As I continued to ignore it, the desire morphed into an order. At least I am no longer wandering directionless, I thought. I had a direction to move onward with, but still nowhere to call home. I continued forward past the bridge that pointed to the place behind me. That day, I left Aigaion.

Chapter 4

I needed strength. I had a forgotten goal I needed to achieve. I continued to think one day it would come back to me, but by the time I entered a neighboring village the thought still had never arrived. After the guards at the gate allowed me in, the village that greeted me felt so much more normal. The strangers that passed paid no mind to me and not a single person spoke a word. I felt more comfortable in this village that met my expectations, Dodasa.

I rested briefly on a bench as I ate the bread given to me. As I carried on towards the military office, I observed how different this place was opposed to the place I woke up. Clouds covered the sky. Tall fences guarded each establishment from the people beyond. No one outside did anything besides walking to their next destination. When I entered the military office explaining that I would like to train and fight with them, they asked for my name. I knew I had to give an answer, so I gave them the only syllables that came to mind, "Hera."

"And family name?" the intimidating woman asked.

I replied honestly this time, "I don't have one."

"Orphan?"

I gave her a quick nod.

"Well, we will take anyone as long as you won't hinder us." She explained.

The woman told me to come back tomorrow for a fitness test, then I exited. Soon, it dawned on me I had nowhere to rest. I stood penniless and alone observing if any strangers would open their doors to me, but I continued to be ignored. Eventually, I traveled outside the gates and camped out in the woods near the walls. In the morning I resumed eating the bread left. Then, I arrived at the office determined to prove myself.

I followed the instructions given to me and performed as best I could to prove I would become a good warrior. After I completed ever task the examiner gave his verdict, "You'll do." Those were his only words. I left that day with a uniform, instructions, and a key for a room at the military training sight. I finally had a place I could stay, but I could not call it my own.

Across from my bed stood another with a mid-aged woman on top. She introduced herself as Daphne and rarely spoke to me after. I woke up every morning and participated in training for Dodasa's army. I listened to their instructions, put my upmost effort into gaining strength, and followed them into their wars. However, they looked down on me as an outsider with no family name. They hated it when I spoke or when I suggested alternative methods, so I spoke to no one. I looked up to no one. I grew stronger for no one.

Often, I sat alone at my desk trying to remember my goal, the reason I desired strength so much. Despite my persistence, my reason never revealed itself. My will never dulled though. I worked twice as hard as my peers. I surpassed them in work ethic. I pushed passed the physical tolls, so that I would no longer be looked at as weak. I always returned from the wars because I still needed to do something unforeseen to me. No longer would I be tossed aside or seen as unworthy to fight.

I trained so hard every day, my whole body ached in pain, but it was worth it for the goal that was still hidden from me. I became known as one of the strongest warriors in Dodasa's army, but that did not mean I would always be needed. After Daphne retired after years of service, I got a room to myself. Soon, my body started to imitate hers. I stopped improving, but instead started to decay. I got slower, weaker, and my bones crackled. I kept rejecting retirement, but one day they told me to pack my bags and ordered, "Hera, go home."

"Where," I thought. As I packed my belongings, I found stuffed deep in my bag a mechanical toy. It surprised me and gave me a new activity. I tore it apart and reassembled it with ease. I glanced at it every day wondering its origin. I began tinkering again as an old hobby that used to be a habit. I made more toys out of spare rubble, fixed the door hinges where I rented, and even made miniatures of weapons that popped into my head. I filled my small apartment with a variety of inventions and at my desk existed a display of a walled off village across a bridge that I made. However, every invention I made sat unused.

My mind haunted that room. I desired to get stronger, but I could no longer physically fulfill that request. The best I could do was create and innovate to improve what I could. However, Dodasa's people saw me as a shut in and refused to know any outsider. Even when I possessed the confidence to offer assistance with my inventions, they shouted at me to leave them alone. I grew more and more isolated, till a knock at my door intruded into my ears.

I thought I heard wrong. Maybe something fell or the sound came from a ghost. I ignored it, but eventually another knock came louder than before. Then, the sound repeated until the door opened. The intruder was a tall young woman with long black hair and a hood that covered her eyes. Her clothes were completely strange, but she composed herself with confidence. She told me the story of a little girl who saved a hopeless village but ended it before the happy ending. I told her that the story needs a conclusion where the girl comes home to the village, and they celebrate the miracle? The young storyteller replied, "Then come with me then," she continued, "You have been gone from your home too long now!?"

STRENGTH
STRENGTH
STRENGTH

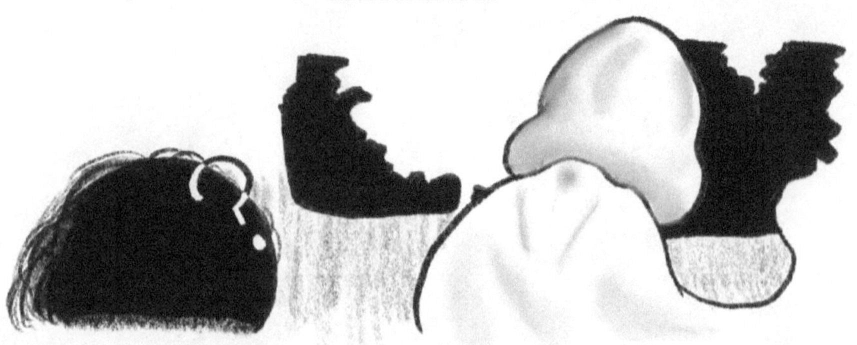

I went with her out of curiosity and on the way, she slowly revealed more things about the girl. "She was an inventor. She lived with the blacksmith and his family. She wasn't raised in the village but called it home. Just as she rescued the village from its oppressors so did the village for her. She considered everyone there her family!" Then she said, "Her name was Hera!" We walked into a wilted gloomy land. The stranger and I entered through an open space in the large, cracked stone walls. There were many buildings but no people. With tears in my eyes I exclaimed, "I failed, I'm sorry, I failed to protect my home!" I wasn't talking to the hooded lady. I was apologizing to the me I forgot.

We approached a small, fenced area with many engraved stone tablets on the ground. This place appeared to be the only maintained area within the walls. "Colin," "Dimitris," "Ajax," "Eleni," and "Evander," all appeared on a plaque. In front of Evander's grave, my friend that took me in and who became like my father, stood a family. A man stood in front at the two graves holding his children's hands, telling them about their grandparents. Eventually, he turned around and faced me. His children stepping behind him. he told them in a soft voice, "Don't be afraid. She is your aunt who saved my village." He looked at me with a smile and tears in his eyes, "Hera?"

I still barely had any memories, but I knew that he was family. His children called out to me, "Auntie, where have you been?!" I stayed silent. Then their father answered, "She's been here, watching over the village even after everyone has gone!" He approached me and said, "Your family, I grew up hearing my parents talk about the sister I had, and they knew you would return to see them."

One of his children clutched my hand, "Come home with us!' She ordered. Then, I answered, "I will. I promise I will never leave my family again." We walked together past all the older buildings and through the entrance. Just before we left, I turned to the lady and comforted her, "You didn't fail, here is your happy ending." Then I went home to meet my family once more with Helios.

AJAX

Epilogue

"Take me with you!" I volunteered. Mom rushed over to release my hands off dad's coat.

"It's a long walk," he stated.

I returned to tug on his coat anyway, "I wanna see grandma and grandpa too!"

He relented and took my hand. "Do you want to come too?" he asked Evan, my little brother.

"No," he said simply as he played with dad's old toys.

He's too young to notice the change in dad. At Evan's age, dad took me to a run-down village where my grandparents lived, his home. My mom wouldn't let me speak as dad did his work. He approached the gravestones one by one and swept the dirt away. As he carefully scrubbed each name, he'd pray. Mom would pack lunch and the three of us would sit as dad told stories of each of the names. He took pride in his history and told many heroic tales. However, he always tried looking for something that never appeared. Often, he would stop tales prematurely to survey the area once more. I wanted to ask questions, but mother always stopped my words.

Sometimes, he would mention his sister, but those stories always ended quickly. Dad praised her as the biggest hero of all time. As early as he can remember, he has always looked up to her. Although, all his stories of her were told to him. His eyes lit up recalling his parents speaking of her. I did not know if she was real or just another tale, but I knew he loved her. All the toys he gave us were supposedly made by her. Dad took pride in the fact he never played with any other toys growing up.

Grandma and Grandpa stopped mentioning her after my dad heard them speak as if she was dead. He kept repeating to them that she never died. He reacted as a child learning the tooth fairy was not real. It created a divide between him and his parents for a while. During that time, he would only keep watch over the village from the bridge to avoid his parents. One day, I came with him out of curiosity. We let our legs dangle off the bridge till Dad forced himself to go home. I realized dad had incredible patience then. Eventually, they all reaffirmed their promise to wait for her to come home. It's sad they could not live long enough to fulfill that promise.

Dad held my hand tight, the same way as when crossing the bridge, while we visited their graves. I understood now why mom did not want me to come. It felt different standing before the graves knowing the name displayed personally. I only knew them by their alias of grandma and grandpa, but the names dad cleaned read Evander and Eleni. My middle name is Eleni, and dad named Evan after Evander. He wanted to keep their memory alive with us, now I know why.

After both his parents died, my dad adamantly decided we all would move into his parent's house. Mother refused to move because she didn't want to live in an abandoned village. Despite dad's persistent pleas, mom won the argument, so dad began visiting their house daily every night after supper. Today was the first day I came with him. I hoped to do something to lift his spirits. Suddenly, dad held my hand closer and turned around. He heard footsteps before me. A hooded young lady approached us and told my dad, "I'm sorry to disappoint."

"Leave," he immediately replied.

"I came to apologize to them one last time," she informed.

"Your apology is not accepted!" he shouted at her.

"I did all I could."

"Liar!" he shouted again. "She's still out there. I know it and you know where she is."

"I can't just-"

"Stop making excuses and go get her," he interrupted.

The lady briefly glanced at me and replied, "Bring both of them tomorrow," as she left.

Dad couldn't sleep that night. I heard him get up and pace for hours. In the morning he took both Evan and I by the hand, after kissing mom goodbye for the day. Sleepy Evan wanted to go back home after walking awhile, but I gestured for him to keep going. Dad only paused on the way when we got to the bridge. We stood there staring at the stone walls for a bit, before continuing to the graves.

Dad couldn't stop talking this time and told Evan all the stories he told me before Evan was born. This time the stories focused on his family unit of his dad, mom, and sister. I didn't know her name. Dad insisted on always calling her his sister to make their relationship clear. I never heard him say her name, until the stranger from yesterday approached with another. Evan and I hid behind him, but he urged us to meet the new stranger. "She is your aunt, who saved my village," he said.

Then he spoke a word I did not expect, "Hera." I glanced up at him realizing he was referring to her. Evan approached her and immediately called her, "Auntie." When I approached her, I grabbed her hand and demanded, "Come home with us!" As the four of us walked home together, I introduced myself. "My name is Hera too!" I smiled. She smiled back and glanced at my dad. He explained, "Evan's middle name is also Helios. I loved the names given to us by our father."

EVANDER
ELENI
HERA
HELIOS

About The Author

Riza Lubasheva, an American author, half Australian and half Filipino. Riza grew up in Texas and works as a writing tutor. Her love for creating stories drives her to write and illustrate her ideas. She also helped raise a cute dog, who looks a little like a rat, named Sonny.